Hotwife Finds Pleasure With Her Husband's Friend - A Hot Wife Multiple Partner Wife Sharing Romance Novel

Karly Violet

Published by Karly Violet, 2020.

This is a work of fiction. Similarities to real people, places, or events are entirely coincidental.

HOTWIFE FINDS PLEASURE WITH HER HUSBAND'S FRIEND - A HOT WIFE MULTIPLE PARTNER WIFE SHARING ROMANCE NOVEL

First edition. December 7, 2020.

ISBN: 979-8201254131

Written by Karly Violet.

Hotwife Finds Pleasure With Her Husband's Friend

A Hot Wife Multiple Partner Wife Sharing Romance Novel

Author's note: All character in this story are 18 years of age and older. This is a work of fiction, any resemblance to real live name or events are purely coincidental.

Be aware: This story is written for, and should only be enjoyed by, ADULTS. It includes explicit descriptions of intense sexual activity between consenting adults.

Note that this work of fiction resembles a fantasy world, all events taking place are a result of a role play amongst all parties and all parties are fully consenting adults.

Sign up to my Patreon account and receive exclusive Hotwife stories every month and sexy scenes every week!

https://www.patreon.com/karlyviolet

Chapter One: Soviets and Sake

Colonel Allen Markham has aged well over his forty years and I feel myself a bit outclassed in our conversation as we enjoy plates of sushi and small cups of sake together.

"It was a damned dangerous thing to do," I tell him as I put down my empty cup of sake. "The whole NATO exercise could end up causing a military confrontation in Eastern Europe, Allen."

The colonel scoffs as he shakes his head. "Look, I understand the CIA is balls-deep in the whole thing now, but surely you don't think that you have the cajones to go toe-to-toe with the Pentagon over this, Sean. We know what we're doing over there. There won't be a war with anyone anytime soon."

"It's nineteen-eighty-three," I reply. "Andropov may not be Brezhnev, but he's also not a kitten to be toyed with. Colonel, you do get that the Soviets are now on high alert, don't you? That's not something that our friends in Western Europe want to see happening. As a matter of fact, it scares the shit out of most of them."

"They are all in NATO," Allen replies. "It was simply a few exercises, Sean. I can't help what optics the Soviets wish to use when they see that sort of thing."

"A few exercises with *nukes.*" We are both quiet for a moment as my comment sinks in. The United States led NATO in a plan to have nuclear maneuvers undertaken near the U.S.S.R.'s Eastern European interests. Although the intended message in the maneuvers was that we would not allow them to make any unilateral incursions into their neighbors, they have certainly not gotten precisely *that* message. The problems in Poland have also not helped at all.

"Sean," Colonel Markham begins while looking into my eyes. "We have things handled. The administration is working on diplomatic channels with the Soviets and they appear to be receptive to talking. Even Andropov is considering coming stateside to hold meetings with Reagan."

"Shit," I say while shaking my head. "That's not something I want to happen. Could you imagine what sort of fuckstorm it would bring upon us if Andropov were to drop dead while over here? The man is not healthy, Allen. The Politburo in Moscow would claim that we poisoned their leader. It could be a pretext to something in Europe like the full invasion of Eastern Europe."

Allen laughs. "Sean, you have had your head down in the intelligence reports at the agency for far too long now. How long have you been with them?"

"Eight years," I reply. "One of the youngest analysts ever when they selected me," I remind him proudly. "I know what I am seeing in the reports, Colonel. Things are not going well over there."

"And you're what, thirty?"

"Thirty-two," I reply. "What? Are we going to compare our dicks next?" We both laugh as I reach for the small white bottle of sake. Pouring myself another tiny cupful, I take a drink and enjoy the warmth of the Japanese rice whiskey. Colonel Markham and I have been meeting here once every week for the last two years. Ever since I was made liaison to the Pentagon, I have seen myself grow closer to the attache to the Strategic Defense Committee. It is important to be well-connected for the good of both government bodies, but more so for the CIA's own goals.

"There's a lot of shit that goes on in the real world, Sean. The agency surely sees that. It's not our fault that the Ruskies took things a little too literally. They know we have drills in Europe three times a year, and honestly, it's none of their fucking business."

"Well, they seem to highly disagree with you," I say with a strained look on my face. "A fire was started and we need to cool it down before NATO gets its feathers singed."

"Fine. We're trying, alright? You need to go back and tell that to Sheffield." My direct supervisor, Bill Sheffield, is not happy about what our intelligence reports have been telling us recently. The Soviets have been working hard to crack our secret networks in their country, and the fact that there are war games going on in Europe with nuclear weapons has intensified that effort. We have important contacts in the Kremlin who are vital to our understanding of what the Soviets are doing. Risking them because of some fucking show of strength has made the CIA very nervous. The Pentagon, however, is only worried about showing our Cold War enemy that we mean business.

"Yeah, I know, Allen." Sighing for a moment, I ask, "How's Monica?"

Colonel Markham raises an eyebrow. "And now we talk about the wives? Is this CIA business as well?"

"I'm pulling off my agency hat and putting on my personal hat, my friend. Has everything been going alright between the two of you? I didn't see her at the last event the State Department held."

Allen sits back in his seat. "We're still married," he replies flatly. "That's something, right?"

"I suppose so," I answer while nodding my head. "But there is more, huh?"

"More *shit,*" Allen says with a grimace. "Monica used to be a sweet, warm woman, Sean. For the last few years I have watched her become more and more distant with me. We don't even get anything going in the bedroom anymore." The colonel crosses his arms across his chest. "I barely see her anymore, Sean. She stays with her sister in Oregon most of the time."

"Wow, all the way across the country? Does she hate D.C. that much?"

He shrugs his shoulders. "She never liked Washington to begin with. We moved here and as soon as we did things began to cool with us. Maybe I should have turned down that position in the Pentagon, but it was a real career boost. Monica said she was fine with it all, but I think she was probably lying. She wanted me to be happy, but then ultimately she couldn't find that happiness for herself. It's the reason that I don't complain when she wants to go stay with her sister on the Pacific coast for weeks at a time." Allen is obviously unhappy with his current marital situation. I can only imagine how hard his personal life has become.

"You should come to the next gala," I tell him as I change the conversation to something happier. "Carrie says this will be a huge one and the Soviet ambassador will be there. I think it's one of the ways they are trying to assure them that we are not trying to set them up for a fast nuclear attack. Maybe you can come over and use some of your Russian language skills to mingle."

"My very *rusty* Russian," the colonel replies with a chuckle. "I probably sound like a New Yorker trying to use a southern accent, Sean. It's embarrassing, really."

I laugh. "Well, come to the gala and meet some of the people there. Carrie swears it will be a great time."

"Ah, your lovely wife," he replies. "She is still very busy, isn't she?"

I nod my head. "Busier than I would sometimes like, but that's what she chose to do when she became the head event planner for the State Department. There have been a lot of long days in which I have barely seen her face before going to work."

"That's tough," Allen says as he sighs. "Don't let this city eat you both alive, man. It's not worth the damage it can bring to your marriage. You need to get out of here with her once in a while. Besides, she's got to be great in bed."

"What?" I laugh a little while shaking my head.

"Oh, hell, Sean. I've seen her legs. I'll bet she can nearly snap you in half with those." We both laugh, though I think my laughter is less at ease than Colonel Markham's. He finds things funny that most other people would take offense at.

"She works out more than I do on most days," I admit. "Carrie is a very physically fit person. If only I had her dedication."

"If only Monica had her body and a better attitude." Again, we both laugh. It is good to see my friend find a little humor in what has been going on in his life. This willingness to be happy even in times of deep trouble is why Colonel Allen Markham is such a special part of the Pentagon. He can remove himself from his troubles to be honest with the command there when a true assessment is needed.

"So, come to the gala next weekend," I tell him. "You will have a great time."

"Yeah, maybe I will." He finishes his sake and raises his hand. Our server comes to the table quickly. "I'll take the ticket, please."

"I've got this," I say as I look at both men. "Allen, you paid for it last time."

"I'm feeling generous this time," he answers while signing on the ticket. "Besides, I have a standing account here. I'll get the bill at the end of the month." The server bows slightly after taking the signed ticket and walks away.

"An account? Seriously?"

"The Pentagon is an important customer throughout the D.C. area, my friend. We can get accounts for anything."

"So, this isn't your personal account?" Colonel Markham simply laughs as he stands up from his seat. He reaches for his military suit jacket and puts it on as I get up from my own seat. After putting on my own dress jacket, I walk out of the restaurant with the colonel and we begin to walk along the sidewalk.

"Thanks for lunch," I reply. "You really, or the *Pentagon* really, shouldn't have paid for it."

"You are very welcome, Sean." He stops and adds, "I'll try to get to the gala that evening. Just make sure your beautiful wife is there. She's easy on the eyes, my friend."

"Oh, hell, Allen." We both laugh as we shake each other's hands. The colonel turns and walks along a different sidewalk and I continue on my way back to my office. Though we could have caught a taxi or even had drivers from our respective government offices take us to and from the restaurant, walking helps to clear our minds. There are a lot of different things that we each have to be concerned about in our individual careers.

The situation has gotten much more difficult with the Soviet Union's decision to take the NATO exercises so seriously. Though I see it all as a collective fuck-up, Colonel Markham's colleagues at the Pentagon have a metaphorical woody for a dustup with the Soviets. Though not wise and possibly problematic for the rest of the Washington, D.C. establishment, we will have to let things play out for now. If NATO is smart, they will back off and put the nukes away. Otherwise, the shit there could hit the fan very soon.

Chapter Two: An Important Event

"That was a tall order," I say as I look at the file folder on my wife's office desk inside our den. "Damn, this looks like a logistical nightmare, honey."

"Not really," Carrie replies with a soft smile as she pulls the folder from my hands and puts it back down on the desk in front of her. "I've gotten pretty good at this over the last couple of years. It's really easy once you get your footing."

"More than two hundred dignitaries and their guests? That's going to be a huge bash."

"It has to be," she replies. "It seems that the CIA and the Pentagon's intelligence arm are not so...*intelligent* after all." Carrie's blue eyes sparkle as she smirks while looking up at me. I married my beautiful wife eight years ago after she graduated from New York University. She then transferred to George Washington University for her masters and doctoral degrees in geopolitics and I barely saw her for about three years. We were two driven professionals throughout our twenties and now that we are beginning to see our thirties dawn, we are enjoying the fruits of our labors. My wife was highly sought after by the State Department when her current job title opened up. She was undoubtedly the best choice they had out of all the candidates who interviewed for the position.

"You know, you don't have to knock the CIA," I reply. "We had nothing to do with what NATO did in Europe, honey. The Pentagon could certainly be held to account, though."

Carrie laughs. "I know how the agency works, Sean. They are constantly looking at how they can interfere with what other governments are doing. This time, you guys have gotten your dicks caught in the door because of NATO."

"Our dicks in the door?" I laugh hard as I look down at my wife. "Where did you get that mouth from?"

"Mostly my father," Carrie answers with yet another smirk. "He couldn't stand the CIA either."

"He was a great operative, you know?" I reply. "He really wanted you to join the agency."

"It's not my cup of soup," she answers. "Besides, they like to suck your soul out of your body and then spit what's left of it out. The State Department is a much better fit for me."

"So that you can design parties? Come on, Carrie. You should apply to the agency. I can put a good word in for you too."

She shakes her head. "They wouldn't let me work here in D.C. with you, Sean. You know they don't like to mix personal and professional lives that way."

"There are plenty of other husband and wife couples in the CIA. Besides, we would probably never see each other during the day anyway."

"Thanks but no thanks," Carrie says while shaking her head. She has gone back to looking at the content of the file folder again as I take a seat nearby. "Besides, I get to meet some pretty incredible people next week at the gala."

"Oh, really? Like who?"

"I thought you would already know, sweetheart. After all, the CIA knows everything, right?" Carrie loves to playfully poke at me whenever we have these sorts of conversations. She knows that I am a bit sensitive to someone speaking ill of the agency, and she also understands that I have a very difficult job.

"There were some intelligence briefings about it the other day, but I guess I forgot to attend." My wife giggles at my humor and I look out at the sun setting in the west. "What a day it has been. Please tell me the right people are coming to this thing, Carrie."

"Ambassador Anatoly Dobrynin is supposed to be there along with the ambassadors from several other Eastern and Western European countries. This is a big deal and we were told to spare no expense."

"Shit." I laugh as I hear the name of the Soviet Union's ambassador to the United States. "Dobrynin is a firebrand."

"A firebrand and a man who apparently enjoys rubbing elbows with others just like him. The man is a social bug, Sean. If we can schmooze him the right way, he might be able to get his country to back down a little."

"A doctorate in geopolitics and you are a party planner." This sort of comment always annoys my wife. It is not as if I mean to belittle what she does, but I want her to understand just how much more she could accomplish if she put her degree to better use.

"It has served me well in my current job," she tells me as she gets up from her desk chair. Carrie walks over to me and has a seat nearby after giving me a soft kiss. "You do the spy job stuff and I keep the peace wherever I can. I think Ambassador Dobrynin will have a great time. I'm just not all that certain that his boss in Moscow is all that ready to listen to reason. There will likely come a time when direct negotiations will be necessary. President Reagan is best in that capacity."

"Maybe," I admit. "Still, if NATO keeps their fingers on the trigger, Andropov is going to get a little anxious to march his troops over a border somewhere. They don't play around when it comes to Eastern Europe, Carrie. This shindig has to be perfect and we have to play right up to the Soviets. They expect as much, I think."

My wife smiles. "Of course they do. After all, they can't trust the rest of the government to be as accommodating." It is another gentle dig at the CIA as well as the Pentagon for the way the Soviets are behaving right now. She is right, of course. The military exercises by NATO, which included the United States, were meant to get their attention. With the nuclear missiles and other equipment there, it certainly did what they expected in the Pentagon. Unfortunately, that attention has caused serious sabre-rattling near the borders of several European countries, which has further caused concern worldwide that there could be a nuclear showdown there soon.

"Colonel Markham's wife is probably going to leave him," I tell Carrie as I change the topic of conversation.

My wife looks over at me. "Seriously? Monica is leaving?" I nod my head. "Why? They seem to have such a good marriage."

"I thought so too," I agree. "Allen told me yesterday that she stays with her sister in Oregon most of the time. He blames the D.C. atmosphere more than anything else." I think for a moment about the colonel and his wife. We have had dinner with the two of them on multiple occasions, and not one time do I recall the two of them being less than courteous to each other. They seemed to be a perfect couple, full of life and joy. Knowing that their time together is coming to an end causes me to worry about my own marriage in the future.

"I should call Monica," Carrie says as she grimaces. "She needs a friend right now."

"Probably," I agree. "Things have apparently been strained between them for some time." My wife has a caring streak to her when it comes to some people. Allen, though, never was her favorite person. For one thing, she did not care for the rough humor he brought to meals with us. Monica, on the other hand, was quiet and well-spoken. She is more of a fit for Carrie when it comes to personality.

My wife looks over at me. "We don't spend enough time together, Sean. Should we try to do something about that? I don't want the two of us to get to a point where we don't want to be a part of each other's lives." Her blue eyes seem sad as she looks me over. "We both work far too much."

"I know," I reply. "But we do it to make our future much brighter whenever we finally decide to have children, remember? Work hard while you are young and then when you are old you can spend more time with the children. That's what we want, right?"

"Sure," Carrie responds. "How long will that be, though?"

I shrug my shoulders. "I think we'll know when we get there, don't you? We are not like them, honey. Don't allow yourself to think like that. Allen and Monica had issues before now. Sometimes you can't control how you feel about someone, no matter how hard you try to fix things." Little does my wife know, I worry about how we are with each other sometimes. Our sex life could certainly use some improvement, but neither of us know what to do about that. We are professionals with busy lives. Kids and relaxing as a couple has been put on the back burner for the last few years.

"I feel terribly for them," she says while shaking her head. "Speaking of no time for each other," she continues, "I don't think I will be home before midnight, Sean. I have a lot to do about getting everything together for the gala next weekend. Don't wait up for me, alright? I can find my way to bed."

I grimace a little. "Well, don't overdo it all, Carrie. Keep in mind that you need at least seven or eight hours of sleep. You need your strength and lately you have been shorting yourself on rest."

"I know," she replies while nodding. She moves a finger into her blonde hair to adjust it. "I need to get back to work here, Sean. I love you."

"I love you too." I bend forward and kiss my wife gently on the lips before walking out of her home office in our den. There is a lot to consider as I think about the way we have both been working and not spending much time together. I have even begun to have blue balls occasionally as I have tried to hold out from rubbing one out. I could masturbate in the bathroom, and I probably should, but I will not do this for now. Carrie is great about offering to give me a blow job or even a hand job when she comes to bed late at night after working so hard. She gets that a man needs what a man needs, and she always tries to give me that. It is not full sex, but somewhat of a fix to help me keep my horniness level in check. I love Carrie's blow jobs. Hopefully tonight after she gets home she can give me one. If so, I have plenty to offer her as a late dinner.

Chapter Three: Two in the Morning

My cock throbs as I slowly rub the length of it with my hand. Carrie lies next to me while asleep, her breath slow and steady as she enjoys the rest she has sought after a long day.

"Fuck," I mutter quietly as I feel a bit of pre-come form at the end of my johnson. "Carrie." Moaning as I begin to thrust into my hand, I think about how badly I want her. My wife is tired and has had a long day, with a longer one still ahead of her. Waking her from her sleep would be a selfish act, more than likely one that would upset her. Still, I want Carrie. I want to feel her soft, wet pussy around my hard member as I penetrate her deeply.

Looking over in the dim lighting of the bedroom, I can see that my wife is on her back, one arm over her head and the other across her chest. She is naked beneath the satin covers of our bed. It is the way she has slept almost every evening since we married. Carrie rests much better while sleeping in the nude, as do I, so we always come to bed with nothing on. Tonight, though, it is an invitation that is becoming too difficult for me to pass up.

"Shit." I turn and gently pull the covers away from her body. Carrie's well-trimmed pussy comes into view and I admire the landing strip above her clitoris. Bending down, I take in a slow sniff of her musky aroma. I want her. I want my wife.

Pushing her legs back, I bury my face into her small bush and begin to prod my tongue forward to find her sweet lady bit. "What?" Carrie begins to awaken as I eat her clam. "What's going on?" I say nothing as I continue to run my tongue over her swelling clit. "Dammit, Sean, what the fuck?" Though her voice carries an air of annoyance, it is obvious that she is enjoying the way I am nibbling at her nether. Her pussy begins to become wet as it releases its sweet juices. I gratefully lap it up as if I were a puppy being fed for the first time from his mother's nipple.

"Fucking hell, Sean," Carrie moans as her lower back arches and she begins to grind her pussy into my face. "Dammit, I can't believe you are doing this to me. You fucking asshole." Her breathing becomes faster as my wife enjoys the feeling of my tongue and lips on her muff. "Shit...*ahhhhh...*" Carrie begins to orgasm as her lower body moves up and down on the bed. *"Ohhhh, fuck...UHHHH!!!"* She puts her hands on my head, her fingers tussling through my hair as I pull on her clit with my lips. *"Shit...fuck..."* Her small body wriggles around on the bed until my wife finishes coming. I pull my face away and push her legs back so that I can bury my cock inside her wet hole.

"Oh, that's good," I groan as I slide easily into her penis pocket. "Fuck, that's really good."

"You're an asshole," I hear Carrie say as her feet move around over my shoulders. Pretending that I did not hear her, I continue to thrust deep into her pussy. After a few seconds, she says to me, "You woke me up, dammit. Sean, you know that I have an early day tomorrow." Again, I ignore her as I enjoy the feeling of my cock inside her tight hole. Reaching down, I pinch one of her nipples lightly as I screw my wife.

"I'm going to come," I say as I feel my balls tense. "Carrie. *FUCK!!!*" I begin to spurt into my wife's honeyhole as I thrust deep into her small pussy. The head of my cock collides with her cervix, causing me intense pleasure as I empty my white sauce into her womb. *"Uhhh...uhhh...ohhh...uhhh..."* After a few more seconds, I pull out of her pussy and lie back on the bed beside Carrie. Breathing hard, I close my eyes and think about how nice it was to finally get to have sex with my wife. It had been two weeks since the last time we were intimate with each other. My cock was beginning to wonder if it would ever see the inside of her vagina again.

Carrie is quiet for a while before saying again, "You woke me up when I have an early day tomorrow, Sean. That was a little selfish, don't you think?" I turn to see her eyes glaring at me in the dim light of the bedroom. "You could have just gone and finished that up in the bathroom instead of involving me."

"I'm sorry," I say with very little sincerity. "You didn't have any fun while I went down on you?"

"That's not the point," Carrie retorts. "You should have let me sleep tonight. Tomorrow is a busy day for me and I *needed* my sleep, Sean. Now I'm going to have a hard time getting back to sleep." She sits up in bed and then turns to get out of it. Her naked body makes me a little hard as I watch her go to the bathroom. She turns on the light and begins to wash her face.

"I was horny," I tell my wife. "You used to like it when I would wake you up for sex in the middle of the night, honey. You loved to be eaten out like that. Didn't you like it? You came, didn't you?"

Carrie turns to look at me from the bathroom. "Sean, yes, I came. Does that make you feel any better about the fact that you took my sleep away from me? Why couldn't you just wait until tomorrow evening? I don't have much to do the next day and I wouldn't have cared if you kept me up a while longer."

I sigh. "We don't have time for each other anymore," I complain while sitting up on the edge of the bed. "Scheduling sex won't help, either. Not when I wake up and I'm horny for you, Carrie. We work all hours of the week and when the weekend does finally come we often have to be gone for work again. It's like a vicious cycle with us. Why do we let our work interfere with our love life?" This has been a burning question between the two of us for some time now. Working in Washington, D.C. was a dream for both of us, but one that has taken its toll on our marriage. Sex has been hampered by the fact that there are those who need us to do our jobs no matter the personal cost to us.

"You were the first one to take a job that keeps you away all the time," my wife complains while continuing to look hard at me. "The CIA has you working all the time, even on holidays, so it's not my fault that you and I don't get much time off together."

"But, my work is not the only reason," I remind her. "The State Department keeps you hopping all the time with these international meetings and galas. When do you get a break from this? Never. Last Christmas you were knee-deep in that thing with Margaret Thatcher and the Reagans. We didn't even open gifts together until three days after Christmas. When have I not been with you on Christmas because of my work, Carrie?" Bringing this up might as well have been akin to tossing a rock into a hornet's nest. My wife and I had a terrible argument over this several months ago and to bring it up now is probably one of the dumbest things I could have done.

"You won't fucking drop that, will you?" she seethes while walking back into our bedroom. "That was beyond my control, Sean. You know I couldn't have just backed out of that. President Reagan and the First Lady asked me to be there and to make sure that went off without a hitch. I did it and it was a wild success. Why do you still blame me for that? What does it matter that we opened our presents to each other a few days late? It's not like we have kids, Sean. Or wait, are you a child? Is that why you are so angry about something that happened last winter?"

"No, Carrie, I am not a child," I say evenly. "I'm sorry, I shouldn't have brought that up."

"Fucking right you shouldn't have brought it up," my wife spits back as she stares hard at me. "Dammit, you don't have the same respect for my work as you do for your own, do you? That's why you want me to move over to the CIA. You see my job as being something like a party planner and not as someone trying to help build diplomatic relations with other countries."

"I know your work is important," I reply. "Please, Carrie, don't think that I see your work as anything else. I didn't mean to make it sound like that."

"But you do," she presses. "You want me to move to the CIA to work because then I would have an *important* job. Then you could understand why I have to spend long hours and maybe then you would let me sleep instead of waking me to have sex."

"Wait, that's not at all got anything to do with our work, Carrie. I was horny. That's all that it was and is, honey. I was just a horny guy who wanted to have sex with his wife. I'm sorry that I woke you up at two in the morning and I promise that I won't do it again." I turn and lay back down in the bed, pulling the covers up to my head after I do. The whole thing even seems to indicate to me that I am being a little childish, but I would never admit as much to her.

Carrie huffs before telling me, "I have to be up by six in the morning. I'm going to go to the guest bedroom to try to get a little more sleep." I turn to see her walk toward the bathroom to get her robe.

"No, wait," I say as I get out of bed. "Let me." I walk to the bedroom door and open it. "I'm sorry that I woke you up, Carrie. It was pretty selfish of me and I should have kept your needs in mind. Please forgive me." I force a quick smile before walking out of the bedroom and closing the door behind me. As I make my way to the guest bedroom, I think about how little sex we have been having lately. It has begun to have an effect on my relationship with Carrie and I am concerned that it will eventually cause a great deal of angst between the two of us. When we first married, we were sexually active almost every single day. Now, we go weeks at a time without having sex or anything resembling it.

Closing the door of the guest bedroom behind me after going inside, I sit down on the bed and turn on the lamp. There is a small television on the dresser opposite the bed and I turn it on to quietly watch a late night movie on one of the cable television channels. As I lie here naked, I think about what it would be like to just take Carrie and have sex with her at one of the many galas she plans each year. Would I be taken away immediately and charged with some public indecency offense if I were to bend her over a table and fuck her hard? Most probably. Even so, I want to have more sex with Carrie than we have been having and I want it to be the sort of sex that is unbridled and steamy. I am tired of waiting for her to be ready for me and I am even more tired of having to accept just a quick missionary-position fuck in the early morning hours of a work day.

"Maybe I could hire someone to fuck you while I watch," I muse as I think of Carrie and her naked body in the bed. "Maybe he could eat your snatch while I jerk off." My cock becomes hard again and I rub it a little while thinking of such a vulgar display. Something is off with me, at least that is my professional assessment. No ordinary man would want to see his wife with another man. At least, not a man who works for Uncle Sam in a position that is so important.

As I rub my johnson slowly, I continue to think about Carrie with other men. Maybe it is because I have not had much sex with my wife in the last few months that I feel so cheated. Maybe it is because I am truly a pervert. Whatever it is, I can't stop playing with myself as I watch an old science fiction movie on the small television on the dresser of our spare bedroom. I want Carrie to have sex with another man, no matter how revolting such a thought might be to anyone else.

Chapter Four: Intelligence and Stupidity

"Good morning, ladies and gentlemen," Bill Sheffield, my immediate supervisor at the CIA says as he smiles at the group of people gathered in the room. "I want to begin by recognizing Major Landon Holmes, assistant to General Bernard Reynolds at the Pentagon, Mr. Peter Johnston, liaison to the Senate, and Mrs. Linda Trundle, liaison to the House of Representatives. There are others here, including staffers from Congress, the Pentagon, and the White House."

"Who is here from the White House?" Martin Lang, a CIA intelligence analyst asks as he looks around the room. A young woman raises her hand.

"Reesa Charlton, assistant to the Chief of Staff."

"Assistant?" Martin shakes his head. "This shitstorm in Europe with the Soviets surely requires someone higher up the totem pole than an *assistant* to the Chief of Staff, doesn't it?" His eyes focus squarely on the young woman as he shakes his head. "Does the President take this seriously?"

"He takes it very seriously," Ms. Charlton replies. "As a matter of fact, President Reagan has taken briefings twice-daily for the last few weeks on what has been happening in Armenia and Lithuania. I am here because I have been assigned to go through the intelligence word-for-word. I was trained as an analyst as well." Her dark brown eyes do not break contact with the stare of the older man from the CIA. For my part, I admire her strength and resolve in her response.

"Well, it is definitely a shitstorm," Bill Sheffield says to the group. "The Soviets are pretty pissed off at the way we paraded our European nuclear ballistic missile arsenal in their face. In my opinion, we are damned lucky that we haven't had a skirmish along the border yet."

"It's going to happen," one of the legislative liaisons says with a grimace. "Andropov is not a happy camper." He turns his attention to Major Holmes and adds, "What the fuck were you people thinking over there? Are you trying to start World War Three?"

Major Holmes' face turns deep red. "NATO thought it would be a good way to stop some of the sabre-rattling that was already going on in Armenia and some of the other outlying Soviet republics. You people in Congress are full of shit if you think that we can allow a commie country like the Soviets to do whatever they like. They will take over Europe if we roll over for them."

"Nobody is suggesting rolling over," Martin Lang interjects. "Maybe next time do something other than move nuclear missiles near the border with the U.S.S.R."

"Then what the hell should we have done?" the major asks as he stares back at the CIA analyst. "Should we have called Andropov and asked him to pretty-please stop threatening Eastern Europe? Do you think that's the sort of thing that keeps the communist dogs at bay? Fuck me, you people are ridiculous." Major Holmes lights a cigarette as he grits his teeth together. Taking a long drag, he soon exhales a long plume of smoke into the air of the conference room.

"The finger pointing needs to stop," Bill Sheffield says as he looks around the room. "We have to find a way to bring the tension in the region down to something more manageable. There are people in the press beginning to question whether the U.S. government knows what the fuck it's doing in Europe with NATO. Even some of the NATO countries there are shrinking back from withering criticism in their own press. Yes, it's important to keep the Soviets in check, but at the same time we have to avoid provoking them unnecessarily. So, what can we do to cut the tension, ladies and gentlemen?"

As the conversation back and forth becomes more productive, I find myself adrift in my own thoughts as I doodle in my notebook. Carrie was angry early this morning when I woke her to have sex. She had good reason to be upset, as I cost her some very much needed sleep. However, I cannot help but feel a bit sorry for myself as I consider our lack of sexual intimacy lately.

"Sean, what have you been hearing about Armenia?" Mr. Sheffield suddenly asks. I lift my head to look out across the conference room at the other government officials.

"Well, for one thing, the Armenians are protesting to the American Embassy about the positions taken up less than five miles from their border."

"You mean the *Soviets* are protesting," one of the legislative liaisons chimes in.

"Same thing," I reply. "There is intelligence suggesting that the Soviets are considering putting their own short to medium range nukes the same distance from the border on the other side. If they do that, it will cause a lot of concern from not just free Eastern European nations, but for those throughout the rest of Europe. As we know, they have kept their nuclear arsenal a couple of hundred miles back from the border before now."

"How serious are they?" Major Holmes asks after taking another drag from his cigarette.

"Serious enough that they are already amassing a force three times larger than the NATO force that took part in the drills. It appears that the Soviet Premier will likely give the order to move that force into the republics along their western line."

"Not good." Reesa Charlton shakes her head. "The President has been working the phone for the last week to try to get the Soviets to settle down. The problem is, Yuri Andropov is not a huge American cowboy fan." At first, no one in the room realizes that her comment is a joke. Then, one by one, we begin to laugh.

"Are there any Ruskies that are big fans of the Gipper from his movie days?" Mr. Sheffield asks with a smirk on his face.

"Some," Ms. Charlton replies. "But they are in the Politburo and not exactly in a position to challenge Andropov's ambitions. He is very much like Brezhnev was in his attitude toward the west. Though he wants to open up a bit more to have dialogue with the United States and our allies, he deeply distrusts us. That, and not being a huge Ronald Reagan fan, is probably why we have seen several weeks of this problem in Armenia and the other republics.

I sigh as I look over at the young woman. She is attractive and petite, maybe five-two or so in height and just over a hundred pounds. Though not physically imposing, Reesa Charlton is sharp and witty, something that I find highly attractive in a woman. Carrie is the love of my life and my loins burn for her more than anyone else, but if I were to decide to quench my sexual desires with a lover, I would hope that it would be with someone like Reesa Charlton.

"Are all of our nukes backed away as of now?" Mr. Sheffield asks the major.

Major Holmes' face grimaces. "We can't just back everything up with the Ruskies breathing down our necks on the border. Most of our arms have been sent back, but we have a few remaining just in case something happens."

"That is why something will likely happen," I tell him. "You can't just park nuclear missiles on their border and expect Andropov to call off his army."

"It worked with Cuba," Major Holmes muses.

"That was twenty-plus years ago and we nearly went to war, sir," I say as I shake my head. "You need to tell your superiors in the Pentagon that the nukes need to be pulled back."

The major looks over at Reesa Charlton. "The President wants to keep them there. It's not our decision at this time."

She nods her head. "The President has been advised to keep a few missile batteries nearby to keep the Soviets from using the wargames as an excuse to invade Eastern Europe. He wants there to be an equal cooldown from the other side."

"An equal cooldown." I smile at the young woman. Her eyes look me over and I feel goosebumps rise along my neck and shoulders. "I'm not sure Andropov will see the remaining presence of any armaments along their border as equal at all. The President might want to consider removing everything and then hope that the Soviets will respond in kind."

"Or let them just do whatever they want to do," Major Holmes says while putting out his cigarette in an ashtray nearby. "Let's just give Europe to the commies and be done with it. That would make everything so much easier, right?" The strained look on the military career man's face belies the frustration the Pentagon feels with the intelligence community's constant assessment of what is going on with the Soviets. Though they often ask the CIA for intelligence and we also work with military intelligence to a large degree, there is a low amount of respect for the work that we do when it comes to conflicts such as this.

"Ms. Charlton, do you think the President would be willing to withdraw the last missiles from the line? Maybe at least thirty or forty miles back? The effectiveness of the weaponry would not be changed much and the Soviets could at least save some face in the media." Mr. Sheffield looks at the young woman from the White House and waits for her response. My cock becomes somewhat stiff as her eyes look first at me before turning to my supervisor.

"I'll speak with the Chief of Staff and see what can be done. You have to keep in mind that the President is not the sort to capitulate so easily, though. Remember, he took a bullet from a nut case just a couple of years ago. There isn't much that will force him to change his mind unless he feels it is in this country's best interest."

Mr. Sheffield nods his head. "I understand." He looks around the room and asks, "Is there anything else we need to cover before we take a break for a few minutes? My bladder is about to explode after the coffee I had earlier." We all chuckle before he then announces, "Half-hour, people. Be back in here and ready to put together the threat assessment for the President." People begin to get up and walk out of the room. I sit back in my chair and jot down a few notes, not realizing at first that someone has come to sit down beside me.

So, do you really think that we should just back off?" Reesa Charlton smiles at me as she raises an eyebrow.

My heart races for a moment as I move around uneasily in my chair. My cock is now hard as I reply, "I think it's what the Soviets want. Remember, they didn't start this by conducting nuclear drills along that border, Ms. Charlton. We did. It only makes sense that we de-escalate the situation before Andropov decides to march over the border and dare us to do something about it."

"A nuclear war? Do you really think the Soviets would go that far?"

I shrug my shoulders. "Honestly, I don't know. Brezhnev was easier to read when it came to these sorts of things. Andropov is an old KGB guy and because of that he is a harder bastard to understand. All I know is that we have really stirred the pot over there and it would take very little to light that powder keg. One thing that I am certain of is their willingness to engage in some sort of small conventional warfare along the border. They would probably want to get NATO to release one of those ballistic nukes in their direction so that they would have even more reason to seize land on the west of their border."

"I see." Reesa smiles at me. "We should do lunch sometime and talk about this, Sean. I am really interested in your thoughts on this and on some other things related to the Soviets. You could even come to the White House to work some." The offer seems to be a great way to push my career forward, but I also get the sense that there may be more to the offer than I could know.

"I appreciate the offer," I tell her. "Maybe sometime I could come over and see where you work. I have always wondered about the White House and its offices."

The young woman smiles at me before standing to her feet. She extends her hand and I shake it as she replies, "I think you and I could have a great time working together." She then turns and walks out of the room, leaving me to my own vulgar imagination.

"Damn," I say quietly with a quick laugh. "Yes, please." Smiling to myself, I get up and make my way out of the room as well. I could use a little of the coffee Mr. Sheffield mentioned earlier.

Chapter Five: Good for a Few Drinks

We should not be here. Colonel Markham and I are both well known in the D.C. federal establishment and our presence here would be considered an embarrassment to both the CIA and the Pentagon.

"Loosen up," Allen says with a wry smile on his face. "It's not as if I'm in uniform or you are wearing a huge hat that has *CIA* emblazoned upon it."

I allow a tense chuckle as I look around. "When you said that you wanted to take me for a drink at five o'clock in the afternoon, I didn't think that you meant that the drink would be at a strip club, Allen." The large room has three stages and each stage has at least one scantily-clad woman dancing around a pole. This is not the sort of place I would want to be recognized in were there others that I know in the club. As a matter of fact, Carrie would be less than happy with me if she were to discover that I were sitting here having a beer with Allen Markham while gorgeous women show off their wares.

"It's a nice, cozy place to relax, don't you think?" Allen laughs. "Come on, man, just loosen up a bit. They don't bite...unless you pay them." He laughs again, this time his eyes turning toward the stage nearest our table. The colonel watches as a very pretty young woman, her hair blonde and long, swings around the metal pole at the center of the stage. Her eyes meet ours and I turn quickly to look back at my drink. The last thing I need is the attention of any of the dancers in the club.

"She's a very nice one, don't you think?" the colonel asks with a broad smile on his face. "Out of all of the ones here this afternoon, I think I like her the best."

"You're married," I remind him. Though Allen has told me that his marriage is not exactly all that intimate anymore, I would expect him to at least honor his vows.

"And fucking my wife is like fucking a pillow," he tells me as he turns his attention back to me. "I'm tired of being turned down or told that I can do what I want; just get it over with." Allen sighs. "For the last few years I have listened to that woman complain at me and then tell me that she has to go see her sister. She's gone for several days or even weeks at a time, Sean. It's getting pretty old." The colonel's eyes turn back toward the stage as the music stops playing. He smiles at the woman he has been watching. "I think she's coming this way, Sean."

"Oh, shit." I turn for just a moment to see her walking toward us before I turn my attention back to my beer. No, I do not need this sort of attention right now. I need to be thinking only of my wife, Carrie, or about work right now. Another woman cannot be my focus.

"Hello, fellas," the dancer says in a soft, sultry voice. "May I sit with you?" Allen nods his head and I can't help but turn and notice that the woman has no top on right now. Her small, pink nipples are erect on her C-cup breasts as she settles into a chair. "So, where are you guys from?"

"Around here," Allen replies with a smile. "We both work in the city."

"Oh, really?" She looks at him and smiles before turning to look at me. Her blue eyes are brilliant and seem to look straight through me as I feel my face turn bright red. "And what do you gentlemen do for a living here in D.C.?"

I feel my heart pound inside my chest just as Allen answers her. "We are investors with a local firm. I don't want to give you any more information than that, though. If my boss thought I might be sharing financial secrets, he would be pissed." The colonel laughs as he looks briefly at me. He has decided to lie to cover our true identities and he expects me to go along. Of course, being a part of the CIA, I have some ability to go along with such falsities.

"You're quiet," the dancer says to me as she continues to look into my face. "What's your name?" Her hand slowly moves to mine and I feel a sort of shock move from my hand to my shoulder and neck as she rubs a finger along the back of my hand.

"Um, well, I'm James," I lie. "And you?"

"Lilly," she answers me before turning toward the colonel. "What about you, sweetie. What's your name?"

"Chance," he tells her. "It's nice to meet you."

"Very nice to meet the two of you." The young woman turns her attention back to me and asks, "Would you like to feel one of them?" She has caught me looking at her breasts.

"I...um...isn't that *illegal?"* I swallow hard as I look around the room. If I get busted by a cop because I have decided to touch a dancer, my job could end up in the scrapheap of history.

"Only if you get caught." Lilly takes my hand and pulls it to her chest. She places my hand over her right breast, allowing me to feel her erect nipple and the soft skin around it. "Your hand is so warm, James. This is nice." She moves my hand around a little, as if to give me an even greater feel of her nipple. My cock becomes hard as I think about what sex would be like with the dancer. Oh, I would fuck her so hard right now if I could.

"May I?" Allen reaches over and grasps her other breast, enjoying the softness of her chest as I do in the crowded gentlemen's club.

"You two seem to want a dance, right? I could do one or both of you. The fee is not that much more for two."

I slowly pull my hand away from the woman. "That's a nice offer, but I can't do that right now."

"How much?" Allen asks.

"Twenty for the dance with one, thirty for two. It lasts around seven minutes."

"That's a lot of money," the colonel muses. "I think my friend could use a nice one, though. Do you offer any extra services while you are in there with a client?" Allen pulls his wallet out of his pants pocket and holds it close to him.

Lilly smiles. "Sometimes other things can be arranged while we are in there. The room is private and I can lock the door. However, I can't discuss the extras offered out here." She looks around the room for a moment. It is obvious that she is a little nervous to be speaking with two men about paying for things that are not legal in Washington D.C. The vice squad works the clubs daily to discourage such deals on the side.

"What about a helping hand?" Allen says quietly as he smiles at the dancer. "What would that set him back?"

Though obviously nervous, Lilly looks at him and then at me. "Twenty more." Her answer is short and to the point. There is no reason for her to be any more descriptive of what could be expected.

"And a bit more?" Allen asks as he licks his lips. "How much would that set a guy back?"

Lilly, again nervous, says, "Thirty."

"Shit." The colonel smiles as he shakes his head. "I would want full service for that."

"You're kidding, right?" she says with a grimace.

"Well, yeah. I mean, you want thirty to drink through a straw? Come on. You can do better than that, right? We're talking about my friend over here."

"Whoa," I say as I put a hand up. "What do you mean by that?"

"Look, James," he says with a smirk on his face, "You and I both know that you find Lilly very attractive. You've been looking at her since we came in here. Don't you want to experience a little more with her?" The devious look on Allen's face tells me that he is intent on trying to get me to have some form of sex with the young woman.

"You are a handsome man," Lilly says as she reaches for my hand again and squeezes it. She leans toward me and quietly asks, "What would you be willing to pay to put it inside me?"

"Shit."

"Come on, James. What would you do?" Allen's face is red as he smiles at me. He knows this is more than I had bargained for when we came into the club and he is enjoying every moment of it.

"Fifty," Lilly says to me. "It needs to be quick, though. I have raincoats..."

"Wait, he has to wear one of those?" Allen shakes his head. "Let him go bareback until he's ready to pop, alright? He wants to feel everything."

"I can't do this," I tell the two of them. "All I did was come here for a drink. I don't need to go back and do something else." Pulling my hand away from the woman, I sit back in my chair. "Why don't you go back there with her?" I say as I glare at the colonel. "All I want is a drink." The dancer seems confused as she looks into my face.

"Alright, then fifty, but bareback until the job is finished," Allen says to her.

Lilly looks warily at him and then asks, "Will you swear to me that you will pull out before you go? I don't want you doing that inside me."

He nods his head. "I can do that, baby." Colonel Markham gets up from his seat and offers his hand to the woman. Lilly looks one final time at me, smiles, and then leads my friend away to a doorway with a curtain nearby. I sit back and continue to drink my beer.

"Fucking hell," I mutter as I think about what has just happened. If anyone from the CIA or Pentagon were to discover that we were involved in the negotiation of illegal prostitution in this gentlemen's club we would at the very least be demoted. In my case, I could very well lose my position. The Central Intelligence Agency is not the sort of place where the higher-ups take lightly any illicit personal relationships we might develop. The fear that is inherent in the agency is that someone like me could end up bamboozled by some tart and end up giving her important information that could then be collected by the Soviets or another hostile nation. No, going with Lilly into another room would have not been a great idea for the likes of me. Honestly, I feel a bit odd about Allen doing so instead, and I do not know what I am expected to do while he diddles her.

"The bill, please," I say to one of the women who are serving tables. She nods, pulls our ticket from her pocket, and lays it on the table in front of me. I remove ten dollars from my wallet and leave it on the table, part of it as a tip, before getting up and leaving the gentlemen's club. I have covered the colonel's beer tab, which was supposed to be on him to begin with. He is busy, though. Whatever he is looking for in intimacy with another woman, I hope he finds it. That would be better than fucking a pillow, after all.

Chapter Six: Giving Things Another Thought

"Sean." My wife breathes quickly as I pull up her dress and push down her thong panties. "What the fuck are you doing?"

"I need this," I say to Carrie as I slap her ass hard. After bending her over, I spread her ass cheeks and legs and bury my face into her snapper.

"Holy shit, Sean!" Her small body bucks a little as I nip at her swelling clitoris. This was a surprise to my wife after she walked through the door of our apartment after work, but not much of a surprise for me. After coming home from the gentlemen's club I have thought about Lilly and how Allen took her back for some condom-free sex. I wanted to go with her and do that, but I knew how dangerous that could be to my reputation, my job, and to my marriage. However, my balls have ached since then and I need to find a way to alleviate the feeling. Fucking my wife is all I know to do right now.

"You are my little slut," I growl at Carrie as I reach up and try to unzip her small dress. Seeing that the zipper is sticking, I pull at both sides and rip the dress apart.

"SEAN!" My wife turns and looks hard at me. "You're ruining my dress!"

"Fuck your dress," I say to her as I pull it down and look at her soft orbs. I go down on her B-cup breasts, my tongue quickly running along the edges of one of her light pink nipples. Her body tenses as I suck it into my mouth and then release it.

"You fucking asshole," she moans as I sink two of my fingers into her muffin and begin to play with her. "Sean." Carrie grinds into my hand as I massage her clit and move my fingers in and out of her wet hole. The musky aroma of her pussy makes me hard and I soon find myself pulling my fingers from her so that I can get my pants down. As I do, she goes to her knees and takes my cock into her mouth.

"Suck it hard," I plead with her as I put a hand on her head. My wife does as I ask and I wince as it hurts a little. "Make me come, honey. Make me come hard." Running my hands along her cheeks, I feel my manhood move in and out through her lips. Carrie seems to be just as horny as I am now and it makes me even harder as I look down at her torn dress. "Fuck, Carrie. You little slut."

She pulls her mouth from my cock. "You are so dirty, Sean. So fucking dirty." My wife stands to her feet and pulls her ruined dress to the floor. She pushes me toward the couch and I sit down before she goes down on me for a second time. I lurch forward as she rams my cock to the back of her soft, tight throat.

"Dammit, Carrie. Oh, hell, you'll make me shoot into your throat, baby," I say to her as I put a hand on her neck and feel her swallowing slowly. My wife is so good at giving head, often swallowing as she sucks on me so that I get the sensation that my cock is being gently massaged and encouraged to give up its salty surprise. "Fuck, honey."

I get close to coming, but she suddenly stops and looks up at me. "Something got you going, Sean. What did it?" Carrie turns her back to me and lowers her pussy toward my hard shaft. Slowly, she allows her warm twat to surround my pecker as she sits down on me. "What made you so horny?" She reaches around and puts her hand on my face as she rides my cock, her soft back against my chest.

"Oh, Carrie," I moan. "I was just horny for you, that's all. I have wanted you all day."

"Bullshit," she retorts as she grinds into me. "Tell me the truth, dammit." Carrie reaches down and plays with her lady bit as she moves slowly up and down my cock. The way she teases me with her soft, slow movement makes me want to lose my wad, but I cannot just yet. My wife knows me too well when it comes to sex, and she can use it to get whatever she wants from me.

"I got a beer," I say as I strain under the slow movement of her silky pussy along my pole. "With Allen."

"The colonel?" she asks.

"Yeah," I reply as I reach around and feel her small breasts. "Fuck, honey, you are torturing me right now. Speed up a little."

"It was more than a beer, wasn't it?" Carrie says without moving any faster as she rides me. "What was it? Did you go to a titty bar with him, Sean? Did you go look at naked women?" Fuck. She knows. How the hell does she know?

"Honey," I say as I play with her nipples. I can tell that Carrie is getting closer to her own orgasm as well as she runs her fingers along my cheek. She pulls her other hand from her clitoris and lightly sniffs it before putting it beside my face. She knows I can smell her essence now. My wife knows how badly I want to come inside her.

"Did you fuck any of them?" she asks me. "Did you get a lap dance and then fuck one of the girls? It's alright, Sean. Just tell me. I don't care if you fucked one of them." Her small ass grinds into me hard and suddenly I can feel her cervix on the end of my dick. Carrie knows that drives me wild when she forces her cervix onto me.

"Dammit, Carrie. I didn't fuck one of them. She offered, but I didn't do it." My face flushes as I admit what happened at the club. "Please, Carrie."

"Did you want to fuck her?" she asks. "Did you want to fill her full of your jism, Sean? Just tell me. It's alright, my love. I understand." Carrie begins to move a little faster on my cock as she moves her hand back to her clit. She fingers her little nub as she squeezes my cock inside her pussy.

"Oh, fuck..." I feel myself getting closer to coming inside my wife. Do I tell her the truth?

"Did you want her?" she asks again. "I'll bet you would have fucked her hard, Sean. I'll bet you would have emptied your balls into her, wouldn't you? I wish you had fucked her, baby. I wish you had fucked her and came inside her." Her body now picks up speed as I feel myself begin to spurt inside my wife.

"Ahhhh!!!" I spurt hard inside Carrie as I finally release my seed into her. *"Uhhh...uhhh...uhhh...uhhh..."* Over and over again my body tenses as I cream her cervix. My wife continues to move hard on top of me as

she accepts my white sauce into her womb, her body enjoying the feeling of the warm concoction.

"Ohhhhh!!!" Carrie's small body tenses as she orgasms hard on top of me. *"Sean! FUCK HER! FUCK HER!"* She bounces quickly up and down on me as she comes. *"You should have FUCKED HER!!!"* I am shocked to hear my own wife declare that I should have screwed the woman at the gentlemen's club. Though I do not know how she could have found out that I was there earlier this afternoon, she does. *"Nahhhh..."*

Our bodies continue to move together until finally Carrie stops and slowly leans back against me. She kisses me for a moment before leaning forward and getting up off me, a stream of our sexual fluids dripping from her pussy. As my wife quietly sits down on the end of the couch beside me, I cannot help but wonder what she is thinking.

"How did you know?" I finally ask as the silence in the room becomes deafening.

Carrie, still breathing hard, tells me, "I have heard stories about Allen Markham, Sean. Lots of people have. He's been seen at that bar for the last year or so. No one says anything because of who he is." She then turns and looks at me while narrowing her eyes. "You need to be careful, though. I'm not sure your bosses would like the idea that you are hanging out in places like that." Carrie then sits back on the couch and giggles.

"What is it?" I ask as I study the grin on her face. "Doesn't it piss you off that a dancer there offered to have sex with me?"

My wife shrugs her shoulders. "It probably should, but not really. I mean, you're a guy and you get a little on edge sometimes. I knew it was a matter of time before you went to a strip club."

"It's not that I planned to go," I tell her.

"I'm sure," Carrie says with a smile. "But you liked it there, huh? You liked that another woman wanted to have sex with you."

"But, you didn't mean what you said during sex, right? You weren't trying to get me to go have sex with a stripper, where you?" I laugh nervously as I try to gauge what the hell Carrie was up to as we both were in the throes of passion.

"I don't know," she admits. "I know you want more than what we have been having in the bedroom, Sean, and so have I. Maybe there is a part of me that wishes you would just do something like that and get it out of your system. One good romp with another woman might be the sort of thing that gets you to settle down a little. So, I don't know. Maybe." Carrie nods her head as she looks away from me. There is something in her expression that leads me to believe her but at the same time to not believe her. My wife seems torn on the idea of me having sex with anyone besides her, which is why I feel compelled to ask an important question.

"Would you have sex with another man if the opportunity came up?"

She laughs. "Really? Now you are wondering about me? I'm not the one who visited a club, Sean."

"No, but I think you are considering that as well. What if there were a guy who wanted to have sex with you? Would you be okay with that idea, Carrie? Would you let another man have a little fun with you?" My cock hardens a little as I pose the question to my wife. She sees that I am a little horny as my manhood begins to rise.

"Oh, wow, Sean," Carrie begins. "I know you get horny pretty easily, but this is a new one on me. Do you want me to have sex with someone else?"

"Honestly?" She nods her head. "I do. I want you to fuck another man in our bed, honey. And I want to maybe help him with you."

"Help him?" Carrie smirks. "Do you mean that you want a threesome with another man?"

"Sure. It's the sort of thing that I think might get things moving for us again, honey. You and me and a guy we can both trust."

My wife shakes her head. "There aren't a lot of guys either of us know who would do that, sweetheart. Some of them aren't the type that I would want in bed with me."

"There are men out there, attractive and healthy, who would kill for a chance to be with you, Carrie. We can find them. I know we can."

"What are you going to do, Sean? Are you going to use your CIA database to find a man for us?" She giggles. "I don't know about doing that. How would we find someone else, Sean?"

I sigh. "There are men out there. We can place an ad in the paper if we have to."

"That's unseemly," Carrie replies with a grimace. "There's no telling what sorts of men would answer that kind of advertisement, Sean. We have to be careful that we are not found out either. I don't need a scandal and neither do you." My wife shakes her head. "I don't think we can do that, Sean." Getting up from the couch, Carrie begins to walk toward the bathroom. "Do you want to take a quick shower with me, Sean? Maybe have round two while in there?"

I smile sheepishly. "What do you think?" After standing from where I have been sitting, I follow my wife into the bathroom. As I do, I cannot help but think of several men that I know who would probably love to have a chance to screw my wife. Whether she would approve of any of them is debatable, but I am willing to argue for any one of them to be her second lover. For now, though, I will allow this line of thought to rest. Carrie has offered me a shower and more sex. That is all I want to think about right now.

Chapter Seven: Willing Participant

"You know that thing the other afternoon?" Colonel Markham says to me as we walk between two federal buildings near the White House. "That was a little wild for me. I'm sorry if I caused you any embarrassment." Allen pats me on the shoulder as he avoids my brief look at him.

"It wasn't a big deal," I reply. "Maybe it was a little weird for me to see that transaction take place, but at least you got what you wanted, right?" Colonel Markham stops suddenly and looks at a bench near the sidewalk. "Would you mind taking a seat for a moment?" He steps to the side and sits down. I do the same as other people continue to walk past us along the sidewalk. "I really am sorry, Sean. I know that I put you into a tight spot when I took you there and then again when I tried to get you to go with Lilly for a lap dance. It was really very selfish of me." Allen smiles nervously as he looks over at me.

"Well, I know you and your wife have been going through some tough times, Allen."

He sighs. "We haven't had sex in more than three months, Sean. Three fucking months. I have begged the woman for something from her on several occasions, but each time she gives me some kind of excuse. What the fuck do I do?" Allen seems frustrated as he straightens his necktie. Though he has been a strong figure the entire time I have known him in Washington, D.C., it is apparent that his facade is beginning to crack. At forty years old, he is seeing his marriage crumble and his wife's interest in him fade away.

"I'm sorry about everything," I tell him. "I've had my own issues with Carrie sometimes. Thankfully, though, we recently had some better time together."

"Sex," he says flatly. "Just call it what it is, Sean. You get it and I don't. Life isn't treating me quite as well as you." After some thought, he continues, "My wife doesn't want me anymore. It makes me want to give up sometimes, but I haven't yet." The colonel looks into my face and asks, "What if things never get better, Sean? Do I leave Monica? Or, do I just accept things the way that they are and keep my mouth shut?" He turns to look at the people walking past us on the sidewalk. There is a sadness to my old friend and I am not certain what exactly to say to him.

"Carrie and I have begun talking about bringing someone else into our bed for a threesome," I blurt out, surprising both the colonel and myself at the same time.

"What?" Allen raises an eyebrow. "Are you serious?"

"Yeah. We talked about it a couple of days ago. Our marriage, as magical as it might seem to some outside observers, hasn't been all that perfect, you know? We have our own struggles and I think we want to do something to bring a new high to our sex life."

"It's not the seventies anymore," he quips. "You can't just go be swingers like they did then."

"We aren't talking about swinging, Allen. We want a third person in our bed and I think that you might be a good one to have." I stop for a moment, wondering if what I have said will cause my old friend to freak out.

"Wait," he begins while narrowing his eyes at me. "Are you bisexual, Sean?"

"Fuck no," I reply with a chuckle. "I want another man to *help* me with Carrie in bed. I'm thinking that you would be the perfect guy to do that." My heart practically leaps into my throat as I see the expression on his face. Allen Markham, as insistent as he was a few days ago to get me to have sex with Lilly at the gentleman's club, is not the sort of man who so cavalierly agrees to new opportunities in his personal or professional life. I have seen him in meetings with the CIA and the Pentagon weigh out the options before responding to those who want to move things into a different direction. I can tell that he is weighing things out right now while thinking of what my offer means.

"My wife would be really pissed," he says after a moment of thought. "It's one thing to hide someone like Lilly from Monica. I mean, it's one time and done. Move on. Someone like Carrie, though, I know her through you, Sean. Doesn't that make you feel a little weird to make the offer the way you have?"

"Well, I suppose that's a fair question," I reply. "Maybe it is a little weird for me, but at the same time I know you. It keeps us from having to go looking for someone else whom we do not know, right?"

"And your wife is fine with this? She wants *me* to be the third wheel on this tricycle of love?" The colonel laughs a little as he shakes his head.

"She doesn't know just yet," I reply. "We have only talked about doing something like this together. We haven't come up with names yet."

"Shit." Allen shakes his head. "I don't think Carrie will be happy with me in this threesome thing, buddy. You and I both know her well enough to know that she doesn't like me very much."

"You really don't know her as well as you think," I reply. "Trust me, I can talk her into it. Allen, she is ready for this and I think you are too. Since your wife obviously is not taking care of your needs, maybe my wife can do that for you."

He shakes his head. "You are really nuts, you know that? You're offering me sex with your *wife,* Sean. That's got to bother you somewhere deep inside."

"No, it doesn't," I say honestly. "Maybe it would have six months ago, but things have changed in our marriage. Carrie and I need something different in our lives, Allen. You can give us that and make all three of us very happy. So, what do you say? Would you like to try my wife on to see how she fits?" I smile wickedly as I look over at the colonel.

He moves around in his seat while digging around at the front of his pants with his hand. "Dammit, Sean. You just had to say it that way, didn't you?" Allen grimaces a little while also allowing a smile. "You are okay with me sliding my dick into Carrie and fucking her? Without a rubber?"

I shrug my shoulders. "I don't know about the rubber thing. We might have to talk to my wife about that. I'm good with it if she is, though." After a brief pause, I tell him, "If you put her legs back you can get very deep and feel her cervix."

"Fuck, Sean." He wriggles around on the bench a little more. "Is she bushy?"

"Trimmed," I tell him. "Carrie has a nice landing strip that invites her lover to enter her tight, wet pussy. Allen, I think you might really love her pussy." My own cock hardens and I too have to adjust myself to give it more room. The idea of Allen Markham pushing Carrie's legs back and penetrating her with his pecker causes my entire body to shudder a little.

"I'll bet she tastes nice, huh?" he says.

"She tastes better than most. Carrie will give you lots of cherry juice to drink, Allen. All you have to do is run your tongue over her clit and she will be all yours. She doesn't mind a finger in the ass too."

"Holy shit." Allen shakes his head. "You are going to drive me insane, Sean. Stop talking about her." He straightens his jacket and sits up straight. "I can't believe you want me to share Carrie with you, man. This is not the sort of friendship that I thought we would end up with." The colonel laughs about this, but he is right. When we met several years ago, the last thing on my mind was sex between him and my wife. Carrie and I were new to the city and I was trying to establish my career here. Nowhere in any conversation did any of us mention having a threesome. Considering the idea now does seem a little odd, it is actually a little refreshing. I want to see Carrie with another man and I know that Allen is more than up to the job. This could work out very well for us all.

"This is a lot to take in," I say as I fold my hands into my lap. "But, we can do this if you want. All I need to do is speak to Carrie about it. She was primarily worried that we would never be able to find someone we could really connect with in the bedroom, but you could be a lot of fun for her. Anything fun for my wife will be fun for me."

"Alright. Ask her. But if she doesn't want to do this, please don't force the issue, Sean. It's not worth it. Though I appreciate the attempt to get me back into the sex saddle, I don't have to have sex with my friend's wife. There are ladies like Lilly around."

"Yeah, Lilly and fifty bucks."

"Forty," he tells me. "I got a discount." We both laugh as we get up from the bench and begin to walk on the sidewalk once again.

"You know, if Carrie really hates this idea I might need a place to stay for a while. Can you hook me up with a room?"

Allen smiles. "Well, considering that my wife is rarely around anyway, I guess you could come stay with me. I hope it doesn't come to that, though. Like I said, don't try to push anything with her. If Carrie wants to do this, great. If not, I completely understand." He pats me on the shoulder for the second time today. "This is my stop. I'll see you around."

"Yeah, I'll see you soon." I continue to walk as I briefly watch the colonel heading toward his office downtown. Though he works for the Pentagon, they have given him an office and several staffers at a place near the White House. This has allowed him the opportunity to report to the President much quicker than he could otherwise. It also allows him to spend his late afternoons and evenings at the gentlemen's club nearby.

"Well, now to ask Carrie," I say to myself as I make my way to the CIA building. "That will be the trick; to get her to say yes."

Chapter Eight: A Needed Reprieve

Carrie eyes me hard for a few seconds as we sit at our dining room table together. "A hotel? Why would we go to a hotel in the city, Sean? We live here already. That doesn't make much sense."

I came home with some Italian takeout and decided to ask my wife if she would be willing to get away for a while at a hotel in D.C. It is a nice hotel, *The Crest Belleview,* and the sort of place that caters to almost anything we could need or want. Figuring that Carrie would be happy to get away for a night or two, I sprung the question on her while eating tonight. However, I did not consider whether she might question the reasoning for staying there this weekend.

"We need some time away, my love," I reply with a smile. "We stay so busy with our work that we hardly see each other sometimes, so I thought it would be a nice change."

"We live in our own apartment, with our own bed, in a very nice neighborhood, Sean. Why would you want to spend money on a hotel?"

I shrug my shoulders. "We can get away from the telephone and our work." I wave a hand toward a small table in the living room where Carrie has paperwork spread out concerning the recent gala that took place. "You and I can finally have some real time together without being interrupted."

My wife narrows her eyes. "Fine. We can go to the hotel if you want, but what are you up to, Sean? There is something more to this than you are telling me." Her blue eyes look hard into mine and I feel as if she is studying my soul. Carrie has the uncanny ability to read me like a book, so I rarely get anything past her. She is an intelligent woman, full of surprises at times, which is why I was so attracted to her in the first place.

"I want things to be different for us this time," I tell her. "I want to have sex with you in a different way, Carrie. I want to tie you to the bed, blindfold you, and have dirty, unbridled sex with you." My words cause even my own skin to suddenly form goosebumps, so it is not surprising when I notice my wife's small body quiver.

"Sean, that's pretty wild for you. So, you want to take me all the way to a hotel to treat me like some cheap hooker?"

"Not some cheap hooker," I laugh. "You're my wife and I want to have so much more with you, baby. What do you say?"

Carrie nods her head as her face turns light red. She appears to like the idea of having a different sort of sexual encounter with me, but at the same time she seems afraid. Something about this bothers her as she continues to study my face and consider what I am proposing. My wife is not convinced I simply want a round of dirty sex with her.

"What else?" she says firmly. "You worry me sometimes, Sean. The way you try to manipulate things when you want something can be a little aggravating. You're doing that right now, aren't you? This isn't some sort of CIA operation you are trying to rope me into, is it?" I have told her many times before that she would make a great CIA operative. Carrie's mind is so sharp and quick to read a situation that she would be an asset to the agency.

I sigh as I feel my body shake. There is no other way to do this than to be perfectly honest with her. I have to tell my wife my plans for her and Allen Markham. "Just keep an open mind," I begin as I smile nervously at Carrie. Swallowing first, I tell her, "I want to have another man there to have a little fun with you."

Her eyes grow large as she shakes her head. "Are you serious, Sean? Another man besides you?"

"Yeah. Look, I know this sounds way out of character for the two of us, but..."

"Way out of character?" Carrie laughs. "Sean, this is out of character for any normal married couple. You want to have another man with us while I am naked on the bed? And me tied down and not able to leave the room?!" My wife shakes her head as she continues to produce a strained laugh. "Holy shit, you are out of your fucking mind."

"We need this," I tell her. "Our sex life has become a little dull and at times you even get angry at me if I try to initiate something. You know as well as I do that we have to change things up or we are going to begin to drift apart, Carrie. This is our chance to do something that will turn up the heat in our marriage."

"You already have a guy in mind, don't you?" Her eyes lock onto mine. "Sean, you fucking have a guy you want to screw me, don't you?" My cock becomes hard as she confronts me. "Who is it? Who do you want to have sex with your wife, Sean?" There is a slight anger hidden in the tone of her voice as my wife demands a name.

"Honey, I don't want you to know just yet," I reply. "He's a nice guy, clean and very nice looking. You will have a great time with him."

"But you don't want to tell me who it is." Carrie shakes her head. "I don't like this, Sean. Not at all. I feel like you are setting me up for something."

"A threesome," I tell her. "That's something we have talked a little about before, Carrie. "I want to have a threesome with you and I want a man to enjoy you while I watch. It's exciting, right? I can see by the way you are looking at me right now that you are intrigued by this. You want to do this, honey. You are just having a hard time letting go and actually doing it."

She takes a quick breath. "I don't think I can do that. Sean, you are asking me to have sex with a stranger while wearing a blindfold."

"He might or he might not be a stranger to you. I don't want you to know until after."

"Fuck." Carrie shakes her head. "Sean, this is nuts. How can you possibly want this?"

I reach out and put my hand on hers. "You'll love it, I promise. After we have finished you can take off the blindfold and see who it is, but not before. Carrie, do this for us. Do it for me."

"For *you,*" she scoffs. "That's what this is really about, right? You have a dirty little fetish and you want me to help you fulfill it."

"It's your fetish too," I tell her. "You know you want to do this. Just say yes, honey. Take this leap with me and see how much better it can be."

Carrie becomes quiet for a moment as she looks down at my hand on top of hers. We have been happily married for more than eight years, but recently the intimacy between us has begun to cool. We have both blamed our careers for this, but in reality our love life has simply become too stale. Having another person in bed with us could be the answer to our needs. Though my wife worries about who I have selected to be the third person, she knows this is something that we both want. This is something that we both need.

"If I do this," she begins as she raises her head and looks into my eyes again, "What if I suddenly want to stop? Would you stop it?"

I nod my head. "Absolutely, baby. I would never force you into anything. If you don't like what is happening, we will stop and the other man will be asked to leave. It will be over."

"I'll hold you to that, Sean. You know the idea of being tied up already bothers me. I'm more Type A than you think."

"You hate to lose control." Carrie nods her head. "You will have some control, honey. Just tell me to end it and it will all be over. I think you will like it too much to do that, though." Smiling at my wife, I hold her hand tightly inside mine. "Doesn't this make you just a little excited?"

She smiles a little. "I suppose it does, Sean. Sure, we've spoken about having sex with another person, but I never thought it would actually happen. I always considered it just fantasy talk during sex. I didn't realize how much you really wanted to do something like this."

"You are a beautiful woman," I reply. "There are men all over D.C. who would love to have you in bed with them, Carrie. Men who wouldn't need a moment's thought to decide to do that if you asked them. Shit, I'm horny just thinking about it." I laugh as I move around in my chair. My cock is tight against the front of my pants as I think about the colonel burying his manhood deep inside my wife's pussy. Seeing him come inside her will probably make me explode as well.

"You're horny?" Carrie raises her eyebrows. "Who is he? Come on, you can tell me, Sean. You need to let me know."

"No," I answer. "It will be better for you if you don't know. The mystery of it will heighten your pleasure, my love."

My wife allows a giggle. "Yeah, I'll probably take the blindfold off at the end of it all and see that it was just you all the time, huh?"

I laugh. "Well, that would be a disappointment for you, huh? Don't worry, my love; I have a guy ready and waiting."

"Oh, shit," she says as she covers her mouth with a hand for a moment. "You already asked someone?"

"Well, of course. You wouldn't expect me to just grab a guy from the street and ask him to come into the hotel to have sex with you, would you?"

Carrie smiles nervously. "There is a man out there somewhere who you have already asked to fuck me, Sean?" Her face becomes completely red as she considers this fact. "Oh, wow. That's intense."

"He can't wait," I tell her. "He's a really stand-up guy and looks forward to this."

"He *knows* me, then?" I nod my head. "Holy shit, Sean." Carrie quivers a little as she shakes her head.

"It's alright, baby. Like I said, he's a good guy and he's a man who you will love to be with. You will be in good hands, Carrie." I smile as I run my arm along my wife's shoulder. There have been very few times in our marriage that I have seen her so nervous about something. Knowing that the man who will fuck her is someone who knows her is a little worrying to her. Perhaps even a little exciting.

"Okay," Carrie eventually says as she straightens up in her chair. "If I decide we don't do this, we don't do it, right?" I nod my head. "And if this guy turns out to be an asshole in bed, you'll kick his ass, right?"

I laugh. "Sure, I can do that for you, baby. Don't worry." I can see the worry on Carrie's face begin to lift as she looks into my eyes.

"I'll trust you, then," she replies. "This weekend?"

"Friday evening," I say as I smile. "He's ready to be there and the room is already booked. I promise you will not regret this, honey. It's going to be a lot of fun for the three of us."

"The three of us," she chuckles. "I never thought I would say something like that when it comes to our sex life, Sean."

"A threesome for us, honey. A very nice threesome." I lean toward Carrie and give her a quick kiss. My heart, though racing the entire time we discussed this coming weekend, is finally slowing down. Though I thought my wife might refuse to do this with me, she has managed to give in to the fantasy. Friday night Colonel Markham will dip his wick into my wife and I will be there to enjoy it.

Chapter Nine: The Crest Belleview

Carrie looks around the large hotel suite as she shakes her head. "I can't believe that you paid for this, Sean. This is a very expensive suite."

"Sure," I say while nodding. "But it's worth it, right? This is our weekend, Carrie. We deserve to have a nice place to stay."

She laughs. "Yeah, that's what this is, Sean. A nice place to stay."

"Well, and to have sex," I reply as I pull my wife close to me. We kiss hard for a moment as we enjoy the feeling of our bodies together.

"You are a naughty boy." Carrie smiles at me as she taps my cheek with her hand. "I need to shower, if that's alright with you."

"Yeah, that would be great," I reply. "He won't be here for a while and I want to have a little fun with you before he gets here." Smiling wickedly at her, I watch as she walks into the bathroom to take a shower. My cock is hard as my wife closes the door behind her.

"Holy shit," I mutter as I feel a chill run along my back and neck. "This is really going to happen, isn't it?" Rubbing my hands together, I look around the suite and begin to think about how everything should be arranged. Seeing the large king size bed, my cock becomes hard. "The scarves." I turn and walk back to my suitcase and find the scarves I brought with us to use to tie Carrie to the bed. Ropes would have been too rough and I want everything to seem sexier rather than too BDSM. The bed, a Victorian four post bed, is the perfect place to have the sort of fun we plan to have tonight. After tying the scarves to the headboard, I turn and walk back toward the bathroom. I take off my clothes and walk into the bathroom.

"Oh, Sean," Carrie says as I open the shower door and step inside with her. Reaching for the soap, I lather my hands and begin to clean my wife's shoulders and upper back. My cock is stiff as I do this, occasionally rubbing against her soft ass. She reaches back and gently strokes me with her soapy hand and I feel my body tense. Carrie knows just how to get to me when she wants.

"Don't make me come yet," I say as I feel myself getting close to pop. "I want to save it for later." We kiss as we rinse off under the head of the shower, both of us horny and ready for what is going to happen soon. It takes only a few minutes for the two of us to finish up and to exit the shower, the steam hanging thick inside the bathroom. After drying off together, we go to the bed and I show Carrie where I want her to lay.

"I'm scared," she tells me as I begin to tie down one of her wrists. "When will he be here?"

"Soon," I promise. "He will have his own key. I left instructions at the desk downstairs." I kiss my wife on the lips briefly before tying her other hand back. Carrie's small body quivers as she realizes that her arms are secured to the bed.

"And my legs?" she asks.

"I want them to be able to move," I reply with a wicked smile. "We might want them on our shoulders."

"The other man." Carrie swallows hard as I reach for the blindfold. I carefully slip it down over her eyes and then kiss her cheek.

"Be a good girl," I say seductively before going to her chest and kissing on her small breasts.

"Sean," she moans as I take a nipple into my mouth and enjoy the sensation of it against my tongue. "Fuck." She tries to move a hand to my head, but cannot. "Dammit, Sean, I want to use my hands."

"I know," I chuckle. "That's just it, though, isn't it? You want to use your hands so that you can have that control. It's the loss of some of that control that will really get you going, baby. Just give in to it." Just now I noticed someone else in the room with us. Allen has let himself into the room and has begun to take off his clothes.

"He's here, isn't he?" Carrie asks as she moves around on the bed. Her face turning red, she asks, "Can't I just see him and then you can put the blindfold back on?"

"No, honey," I reply. "Just go with this." I nod at the colonel as he finishes undressing. I am a little taken aback by the size of his large cock. As he gets hard, it appears that it could be nine inches of solid meat, which is larger than my eight inches. My wife has always talked about how well-endowed I am, so this will be a real surprise for her.

"Shit, Sean," Carrie says quietly as she catches the scent of Polo on the man beside the bed. I back away and let Allen begin to explore my wife. He reaches down and cups a breast in his hand and she suddenly tenses on the bed. "Oh, shit."

"It's okay," I tell her from the other side of the bed. "I'm here." I watch as Allen bends down and takes one of Carrie's nipples into his mouth. As he enjoys her morsel of breast inside his mouth, his hand moves to her trimmed beaver. The colonel's fingers disappear along the cleft of her snapper and my wife's legs part a little to give him better access.

"Oh..." Carrie breathes hard as her ass begins to grind into the bed. The feeling of the other man's fingers entering her pussy makes her wet and horny, causing my own cock to begin to drip with pre-come.

I stroke my manhood as I watch the two of them together. Allen carefully begins to kiss his way along my wife's soft chest and stomach before he moves her leg and puts it onto his shoulder. Her other leg soon follows and he buries his face into her wet muff. Carrie grabs the scarves around her wrists tightly as she purses her lips together. She obviously enjoys the feeling of his tongue on her swollen clitoris and wants more of him as she grinds into his face. Just as I expected, my sweet wife is giving in to the man whose identity she still does not know.

"Fuck, Sean," she breathes out as her lover laps at ther drooling pussy. "He's fucking good." Allen pushes her legs back and licks from her pussy to her asshole, spending quite a bit of time rimming my wife. "Holy shit...*what the fuck?!*" This is the sort of thing I have tried on Carrie before, only to be stopped by her. She does not like having her asshole tickled with a tongue, as she thinks it is disgusting. However, with Allen now treating her to this, she seems to be changing her opinion on the matter.

"That's it," I say as I get close to the bed. After getting on the bed with them, I let me cock's head rest on one of Carrie's nipples. I then begin to move it around as I pre-come all over her. "Shit, I like this," I say as I run it over her areola.

"Oh..." My wife smiles as she enjoys the attention she is getting from the both of us. "Fuck me," she demands suddenly. "Fuck me hard."

Allen looks at me and smiles before sitting up and pressing his cock against her hole. He pushes into her tight muff as Carrie tenses on the bed. "He's going to fuck you hard," I say to my wife as I get back from them.

"Shit, he's big," she tells me. "Who are you?" she asks him as he begins to thrust in and out of her. "Tell me who you are."

"No," I reply. "He's going to do this anonymously, honey." I smile as Allen grunts a little. He wants so badly to talk dirty to her, but he cannot. The colonel and I discussed earlier what he could and could not do. I want him to come inside my wife before he reveals himself to her.

"He's in so deep." Carrie's toes point hard as she grinds her pelvis into his thrusting manhood. "Is he covered?"

"Covered?" I reply.

"A condom. Does he have one on?"

I chuckle. "He's going to fill you full, baby. Just let him do it." Her face turns red as my wife hears that he is bareback.

"Sean, he should pull out first."

"No," I tell her. "We will quit if you want, but if we do this he's going to come inside you, Carrie." I bend down and whisper into her ear, "He hasn't had any good sex in a long time. He's got a lot in there for you." Standing back up, I stroke my cock with my hand and watch as Allen's balls slap her puckered back door. Will she tell him to stop?

"Shit, you dirty little fucker," Carrie growls as she continues to allow her mysterious lover to screw her. "This feels too fucking good."

Allen's face turns red as he pumps harder and harder. I can see by his face that he is going to lose his wad soon. Even my wife appears to be enjoying this so much that she could climax soon. I am still not certain how I can be a part of this with my wife tied down, but I keep thinking about what I would like to do with her. It could be that I will have to wait for my friend to come before I can get a turn with my own wife.

"Oh..." Allen's body stiffens as he allows the one word out of his mouth.

"I'm going to come," Carrie growls. "Let me see him while I come. Please...*please!!!"* I reach over and pull the blindfold up and over the top of my wife's head so that she can see the man on top of her. *"NOOO!!! FUCK!!!"* She has never much liked my friend Allen, considering him to be self-centered and an asshole in general. Carrie also knows that he is a married man. *"Fuck...ahhhh!!! FUCK!!!"* She reaches up and pulls him down toward her as she looks into Allen's eyes, her pelvis grinding hard against him.

"AHHHH!!!" The colonel comes as he thrusts his penis deep into my wife's womb. Each spurt must be powerful as he lets his gravy flow freely into Carrie's tight snapper. *"Uhhh...uhhh...uhhh..."* He pumps into her hard as he presses his balls hard against her puckered asshole. Allen told me before that he was horny and had not had sex with his wife in over three months. Because of the lack of intimacy he has experienced recently, he delivers a load so large into my wife that some of it begins to spill out from around his large cock. *"Mmmmmahhhh!!!"*

"FUCK!!!" Carrie wriggles around beneath Allen as she finishes her orgasm. *"FUCK!!! SEAN!!!"* Her voice is pitched high as my friend pulls out of my wife and gets off the bed. "Allen? *ALLEN?!"*

"Honey, I told you the other guy knew you."

"Fuck!" Carrie shakes her head as she looks at him. "You came inside me?"

Allen nods his head. "Yeah, I did." There is a slight smirk on his face as he looks from her to me.

"My turn," I say as I decide what I want.

"Dammit, Sean. Don't you dare! You are a fucking asshole!"

"An asshole. Good idea," I joke as I spit on my hard cock and press it against her asshole.

"Don't you do it!"

"Fuck!" Anal sex is not much of her thing, though Carrie and I have done this before. She is a little upset at me that I brought Allen in to fuck her, but I watched as she came even harder when she discovered that he was the one inside her pussy. "Holy shit, baby. You are so tight." I begin to rub her wet clit with my finger as I push her legs far back.

"You asshole." Carrie begins to wriggle around again on the bed as I pleasure her muffin. "You fucking asshole." She closes her eyes and bites her lower lip as I push deep into her back door. Thrusting hard, I enjoy how tightly her sphincter hugs my cock.

"I'm going to come inside you, my little whore," I say as I grip her hips with my hands. "Fuck, you make me so horny you little slut."

Carrie opens her eyes and looks at me before turning her attention to Allen nearby. Her body tenses as she stares at him and suddenly she comes. *"Oh, FUCK!!!"* My wife grits her teeth together as she closes her eyes and turns deep red in her face. *"Ohhhh!!! OHHHH!!!"* Her asshole is tight as she has a powerful orgasm with me inside her.

"SHIT!" I spurt hard as I begin to come as well, and I slap her ass as we both enjoy the intense sensation we are feeling with each other. *"Uhhh...uhhh..."* I pull hard on my wife's ass as I fuck her asshole and wonder whether I might pass out. The sensation is beyond anything I have felt with her or any other woman before. It is my guess that Carrie could say something very similar about her experience as we finish our orgasms together.

I pull out of her asshole and lie down beside my wife on the bed. "Carrie, what the fuck was that?"

Breathing hard, she asks, "Why *Allen?* Why the hell him? He's married to Monica, Sean."

"I'm married, that's true," he replies. "But my wife doesn't really care for sex anymore. I think our marriage is basically over."

Carrie looks over at me. "He came inside my pussy, Sean. Doesn't that scare you just a little?"

"About getting pregnant?" I chuckle. "Wasn't that part of the excitement? The danger of it?" I smile at my wife as she smirks a little. Though she probably won't admit as much right now, it made Carrie horny as well.

"Dammit, Allen. I didn't think I would ever be fucked by you."

He laughs. "But it was good, huh?" He smiles and adds, "I would love to do this again."

"Maybe," I tell him.

"Don't make promises," Carrie chides. "I haven't decided to do that."

"But you will," I reply. "You have to admit it, honey. You liked what you had with Allen a few minutes ago. He was pretty good with you."

Her face turns red. "Maybe."

"That works for me." Allen nods his head at us and picks up his clothes. He dresses and soon has left our suite.

"Let me get that for you," I say to my wife as I reach for her bindings. After untying her, Carrie and I kiss for a while and simply enjoy each other's presence on the bed. So much has happened over the last hour that we need time to process our feelings for each other as well as for what happened. She went along with it, and even seemed to enjoy having Allen fuck her honeypot. I want more, and I think that my wife does too. It could be awhile before I know for certain.

Chapter Ten: A Secret Best Kept

I walk into Carrie's office near the State Department building and close the door behind me. As I have a seat, I smile at her. "How are you doing today, my fine little slut?"

"Sean, careful," my wife replies as she giggles and looks at the windows of her office. "There are other people in this building, you know? You walked past about two-dozen of them."

Nodding my head, I reply, "Yeah, but maybe I want them to know how horny you were this past weekend, my love. Don't you think they would want to know?" I laugh a little as I watch Carrie move a few strands of her hair from her face. "Maybe we could even find another guy for the next go around."

"Uh, no," she says while shaking her head. "I haven't said that I will do that again, Sean. At least, not yet."

"Of course you will," I reply. "You were horny all fucking weekend, Carrie. We couldn't get enough of each other. I still have that hickey on the inside of my thigh." I laugh while pointing toward my crotch.

"Don't tell anyone about that," she says nervously. "You know how quickly rumors spread in this town."

"Sure I do. I work for the CIA, remember?" I laugh before adding, "Honey, I can keep secrets. So can Allen. You don't have to worry about anything, I promise."

"The two of you might be able to keep national secrets, but I'm not so sure about something like this. You both like to hit that strip club sometimes."

I blush as I tell her, "That was once and you know it. Besides, we didn't talk shop while we were there. Allen was too much into one of the dancers."

"And pretty much into me this past Friday," Carrie muses.

Sitting back in my chair, I ask her, "What do you want to do the next time, honey? It's your turn to decide what happens and who it happens with." I watch as my wife's face lights up a little at the suggestion that she will have full control over a future romp with someone else.

"The next time," she says quietly. "The next time, I know exactly what I want to do." Her eyes look hard at me. "You will be the one tied to the bed, Sean."

"Me? Naked?" I chuckle. "I'm not sure that will be all that hot with another man in the room."

"Not a man," she tells me as she leans forward and puts her elbows on her desk. "There is a woman I know, a diplomat, that has a thing for you. She saw you at one of the galas you attended."

"What?" I feel my cock become a little hard. "Another *woman?*"

"She's attractive, in her thirties, and a total flirt. The only problem is, she is married with a couple of kids."

"A *diplomat?*" I shake my head. "That would be really dangerous, Carrie. You're joking, right?"

"Nope. I talked to her this morning, as a matter of fact. She and I have known each other for a few months and I think we have an understanding." My mind begins to file through the people my wife knows both in her private and professional life. There is a list of names that come to mind as I think of diplomats Carrie has worked with, the majority of them men. The few women I can think of are in their forties or fifties, not nearly as young as she mentioned.

"You talked to her today? What did you talk about?"

Carrie smiles wickedly. "What happened this weekend."

I take a quick breath. "You just said that you didn't want that to get out to anyone, honey. Did you really tell her about what happened this weekend?" She nods her head. "How can you be sure that she won't tell anyone else?"

"She won't," my wife assures me. "She's a quiet sort of person, very professional." Carrie straightens herself in her chair as she tells me, "I asked if she had a thing for you and she told me that she did. She was actually very forthcoming as to how she feels about you. Although she is happily married and a mother, she wants to bed you, Sean. She is willing to do whatever it takes to make this happen."

"Fuck." I laugh nervously as I shake my head. "Who is she?"

"Uh, no. I don't think so, my sweet husband." Carrie smiles. "Anyway, here is what she wants. She wants for you to be naked and tied down, arms and legs, and she wants to give you oral sex for an hour or more before she rides you."

"Holy shit." I pre-come into my pants as I shift my body around. "She wants to give me a blow job? And you're alright with that, Carrie?"

"Yeah, I think I am," she replies. "Sean, this is a very well connected woman. She's very stylish and very beautiful. I doubt that you would say no to her if you knew her name."

"But, would I be blindfolded?"

My wife nods her head. "Of course you would. That's fair, right? To blindfold you for the main course before revealing her to you?"

I raise an eyebrow and ask, "What is there that would stop you from substituting some guy for a woman, Carrie? I mean, there are a few gay men in D.C. I can think of that you might bring in as a joke."

"Do you want me to?"

"I'm not gay, so, no."

My wife laughs. "It's a woman, Sean. I swear to it. She's attractive and she says she swallows. I just hope that you are up to it."

"Of course I am," I reply with confidence. "You know I can last."

"Maybe, sweetheart. This diplomat wants to make you come as many times as she can in that first hour. Only oral will happen that first hour and she seems convinced she can get you to come at least four times."

"Holy fuck." I laugh nervously. "I don't think I have that in me, Carrie. Most guys can't come that many times in an hour. We tend to run out." Seeing the look on her face I can see that my wife is serious. *"Four times?"*

"That's the minimum, as per my friend," Carrie says with a giggle. "I want to see that happen. Oh, and don't forget, you have to perform for the two of us again after that hour. So, let's say, at least six times that night."

"Fuck."

"Yep. Get ready." The look on my face must be priceless as my wife looks me over. How the hell can I do what she and her diplomat friend want? Six times in a night? Maybe more? My balls will explode. Or implode. Whatever it is, it cannot be good.

"So, when is this?"

"Friday evening," my wife tells me. "Same place. I hope you are ready, Sean. Your world is about to get rocked." I slowly get up from the chair where I am sitting in Carrie's office and make my way to the door. It was only my intention to stay for a few minutes as I have an important meeting soon.

"I'll see you this evening."

"Yeah. This evening." Carrie winks at me before I leave her office.

"What the hell have I done?" I say to myself with a chuckle. "I created a monster." As I walk away from the office door, I hear the receptionist talk to someone nearby.

"You may go in now, Mrs. Johansen." I turn to look and see a beautiful tall, blonde woman. She stands to her feet and smiles at me before turning and walking into my wife's office. I know her. I have met her on many occasions at galas that my wife has produced.

"The Norway delegation," I say as I take a quick breath. "Oh, fuck." Margarite Johansen is the wife of the ambassador to Norway and reported in some circles to be a sort of nymphomaniac. I have always thought the rumors to be nothing but rumors. Is she the woman my wife spoke about? "Damn, Sean. You are in trouble." There is only one way to find out. I suppose I will have to wait until Friday.

THE END

Don't miss out!

Visit the website below and you can sign up to receive emails whenever Karly Violet publishes a new book. There's no charge and no obligation.

https://books2read.com/r/B-A-GIXE-TSMKB

BOOKS 2 READ

Connecting independent readers to independent writers.

Did you love *Hotwife Finds Pleasure With Her Husband's Friend - A Hot Wife Multiple Partner Wife Sharing Romance Novel*? Then you should read *Wife Swapping Party - A Wife Watching Multiple Partner Hotwife Romance Novel*[1] by Karly Violet!

[2]

Imagine joining a new neighbourhood and welcomed into their warm Swinging community!

Jake and Marty recently moved into an exclusive adulted gated community in an affluent area.

Surrounded by wealth and beautiful people, their neighbours intrigued them - with endless flirting and over friendlessness.

The married couple read this as a welcome and supportive community that came with it's members having financial security. .

---

1. https://books2read.com/u/31KPk6
2. https://books2read.com/u/31KPk6

However, as Jake starts to learn more from his next door neighbours, it is clear there is more than meets the eyes.

There are hints of naughty parties centered around keys involving swinging and wife swapping.

And when curiosity gets the better of Jake..........

....and it's not long before husband and wife open the door to the world of swinging and multiple partners!

This scorching hot 20,000 word novel features a curious married couple exploring the virtues of swinging and wife swapping with their exclusive gated community.

Read more at https://www.patreon.com/karlyviolet.

About the Author

Sign up to my mailing list to receive the two free epilogues for 'A Hotwife Adventure' and 'Hotwife Training' and to stay up to date on all of my latest releases! http://eepurl.com/c3ICWf Sign up to my Patreon account and receive exclusive Hotwife stories every month and sexy scenes every week! https://www.patreon.com/karlyviolet

Read more at https://www.patreon.com/karlyviolet.

About the Publisher

www.ingramcontent.com/pod-product-compliance
Ingram Content Group UK Ltd.
Pitfield, Milton Keynes, MK11 3LW, UK
UKHW042012190726
13854UKWH00005B/2264

9 798201 254131